Cheer

A Book to Celebrate Community

Written by
Uncle Ian Aurora

Illustrated by
Natalia Moore

I want us to CHEER
for the people we know,
the community that helps us
to learn and to grow.
They make our lives better
in so many ways,
so let's CHEER for them all
as we go through our days!

Let's CHEER first for moms.
They help us to blossom.

CHEER for our grandpas.
They make our day awesome!

Cheer for the grannies...
the abuelas...the nanas!

CHEER for the dads.
They all act bananas!

cheer for our brothers and sisters
who are all super cool

and the funny bus driver
who gets us to school.

cheer for police,
firefighters, and more...

the person getting the trash...

the one minding the store.

CHEER for teachers
who teach us to read

and the librarian who has
every book we might need.

Principal

CHEER for the principal who makes
the school run so well

and the janitor who makes sure
the place doesn't smell.

Cheer for our pack,
for our squad, for our scouts,

for our teammates who try
extra hard to get outs.

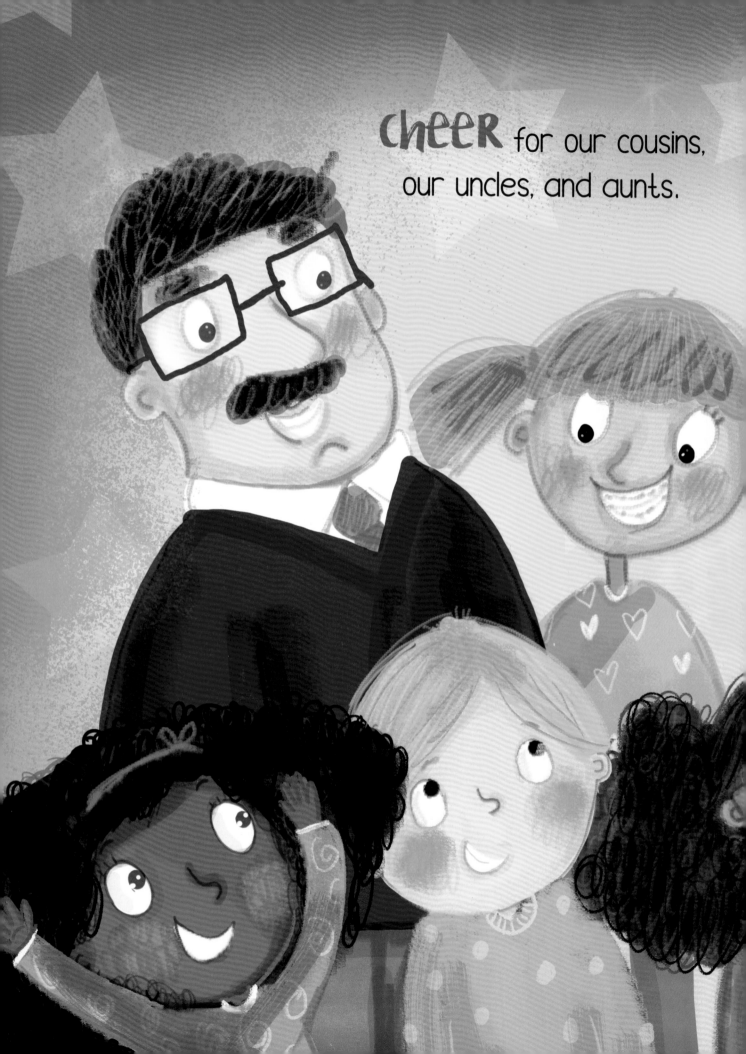

CHEER for our cousins,
our uncles, and aunts.

CHEER for our friends
who join in when we dance!

Now **CHEER** all together
in one big, happy chorus
to say thanks to the author
who wrote this book for us!

These are the people we see every day.
CHEER for each one with the loudest HOORAY!
Working and learning and playing together
makes our communities become even better.
At the end of the day, no one does it alone,
so let's CHEER for them all with a big MEGAPHONE!